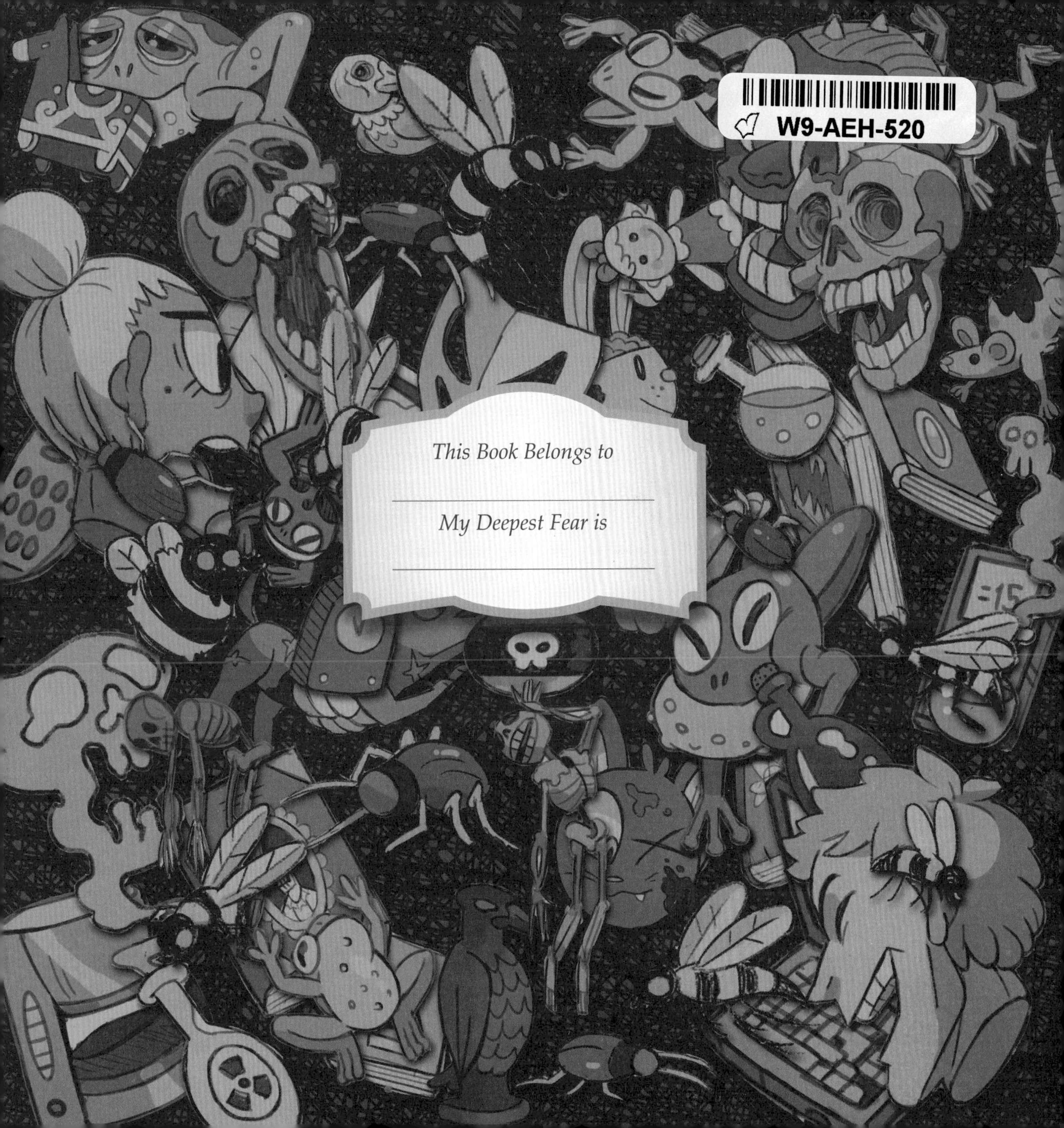

This Book Belongs to

____

My Deepest Fear is

____

=15

=15

AFRAID *of* EVERYTHING

AN ALPHABETICAL COMPENDIUM OF PEOPLE'S WEIRDEST FEARS

WRITTEN BY
ADAM TIERNEY

ILLUSTRATED BY
MATTHIEU COUSIN

EDITED BY
JUSTIN EISINGER AND
ALONZO SIMON

DESIGNED BY
RICHARD SHEINAUS
FOR **GOTHAM DESIGN**

Facebook: **facebook.com/idwpublishing**
Twitter: **@idwpublishing**
YouTube: **youtube.com/idwpublishing**
Tumblr: **tumblr.idwpublishing.com**
Instagram: **instagram.com/idwpublishing**

ISBN : 978-1-168405-627-9 23 22 21 20 1 2 3 4

AFRAID OF EVERYTHING. APRIL 2020. FIRST PRINTING.

DEDICATIONS

To Amy, Django, and Nina
- A.T.

Dedicated to me, Matthieu
- M.C.

CONTENTS

DEAD

GOOD EVENING.

I SAY "EVENING" as I can only imagine you are reading this book at night, which is when all good horror books should be read exclusively. For if the sun is still out, you should go outside to enjoy that sun, and return to these pages later when your house is dark and quiet and unexplained shadows shift about the walls.

What you hold in your hands is a dangerous book... and that's a good thing.

I wrote *AFRAID of EVERYTHING* for my son, Django Tierney, and for 8-year-olds like him across the world who love reading scary stories. When I was his age, in the mid-1980s, horror created for kids was everywhere. We had scary movies, scary toys, scary records, scary cartoons, scary cereal, and especially scary books.

Writers like Alvin Schwartz and R.L. Stine produced clever, terrifying works of fiction that my friends and I loved to read because (and lean in close, because this is a little-known-secret) it's FUN to get SCARED.

But sometime between the 1980s and today, which is a very long time, something changed. Horror for kids was replaced with tamer, sweeter, "spooky" stories that involved ghosts or monsters or Halloween but wasn't really very scary at all. Someone (more likely, many someones) decided that horror wasn't actually appropriate for kids anymore, so it went away.

But here's another secret for you—horror isn't just appropriate for kids, it's ESSENTIAL. Reading scary stories and watching scary movies helps children to become brave and confident, but ONLY when (and this is a big only, which is why it's capitalized) it's produced with them in mind.

Fear, dread, risk, and doom are themes that young readers can handle wonderfully, so long as there is an absence of gore, sadism, and darker themes that are better left to adults.

So please enjoy this collection of (I hope) genuinely scary stories, written especially for young readers, but still quite readable at any age. Blanket and flashlight recommended.

— Adam Christopher Tierney

A is for Arachnophobia

(SPIDERS)

ELOISE HATED HER NEW ROOM. The cracked walls, the dusty floors... nothing felt right.

"You'll get used to it," said her mother, cheerfully folding her teenage daughter's blankets. Eloise noticed a small, wiry spider creeping across her desk.

She smashed it under her fist and sighed loudly. "Not likely..."

The next day after school (which was equally awful), Eloise collapsed into her too-lumpy bed, then noticed a pair of spiders loitering on the wall, inches above her pillow.

"You're multiplying, I see," said Eloise as she slammed her palm flat against them. But retracting her hand, she saw no spidery remains. "Huh."

The next day, Eloise felt horrible. Not just about moving, or about school, but deep in her stomach, as though her internal organs were strangling one another.

Shortly after finishing her lunch (sliced turkey and mashed peas), her lunch decided to return, spewed across the table as a soupy green goop. As Eloise died of embarrassment (not literally), she noticed a tiny, eight-legged gob of peas scurry out of the mess.

After a week of itchy eyelids, peeling skin, and unexplained nausea, her mother took Eloise to the hospital. The Doctor smiled reassuringly (like someone's grandpa) as he fetched her X-ray results. But when he returned, his face looked pale and worried.

Deep inside Eloise's stomach, Nina was hating her new room. The fleshy walls, the veiny floors... nothing felt right.

"You'll get used to it," said her mother, cheerfully spinning a web for her teenage daughter.

Nina sighed loudly. "Not likely..."

B IS FOR Bibliophobia

(BOOKS)

THIRTY MINUTES PAST CLOSING, the lights shut off. It wasn't unusual for Jess to be caught at the library after hours. Her Saturday routine was to grab a pile of books, hide under a desk, and drown herself in stories until she was kicked out.

Jess stumbled through a dark maze of bookshelves toward the glowing EXIT sign. She hoped the door wasn't locked. It was. As she slumped against the door, deciding her next move, she noticed an open hardcover on the floor. Both of its visible pages were blank except for one line: *"Jess picked up the book."*

She flipped the book over. Strange symbols were etched into its leather cover, but no words. She flipped it back over and saw a new line added: *"Jess walked down the hall."*

As she debated doing this, a light above her came on. Jess tried the door again (no luck) then began down the hall. The lights turned on and off as she passed below them. She checked the book. *"Jess opened the door."*

She looked up just in time to avoid bumping into an emergency exit. She opened the door to reveal a dark, winding staircase headed downward. She checked the book again. *"Jess went down."*

The metal staircase was slippery and deteriorating. Jess checked the book but it was too dark to read. She heard a low hum deep below her and spotted a faint red glow, which turned out to be a lamp at the bottom of the stairwell. She held the book up to the deep red light. *"Jess went through the gate."*

A heavy, rusted gate stood before her. She stepped through it. *"Jess closed the gate."* She did. *"Jess took the key."* She pulled an iron key from the gate, inadvertently locking it. She checked the book again. *"Jess tossed the key through the gate."*

She paused, unsure of what to do. Part of her screamed to rush back up the stairs, break a window, and get out of there! But another part of her needed to finish the story.

She stood quiet and indecisive for a long time. *"WELL?"* a voice finally growled from the darkness. *"HOW DOES IT END?"*

Jess screamed, dropping the book. The light went out.

Well? How does it end?

SUPER

C IS FOR Cartilogenophobia

(SKELETONS)

JUST PAST MIDNIGHT (well past bedtime) something woke up Todd.
Something scratched his window as it shuffled through the yard,
Something pale and brittle that was sneaking past his room,
And filled Todd with a mix of curiosity and doom.

Todd rushed to Mom and Dad's room seeking refuge in their bed,
But found a pair of skeletons relaxing there instead.
The skeletons slid off his parents' skin like dirty clothes,
And left their husks deflated on the mattress as they rose.

Todd hid behind a couch and watched them make their pale retreat,
Then followed them covertly to the graveyard down the street.
And there he saw a hundred boney figures congregate,
And chant and dance beneath the moon until the hour was late.

Then as the ghoulish night dissolved between the morning's rays,
The skeletons shook hands, gave hugs, and shuffled toward the graves,
Where they would swap positions with their buried brethren,
To give each undead corpse a chance to rise and live again.

Todd turned to leave, excited to reveal what he'd seen,
But then his skin peeled from his bones and Todd began to scream.
His cries were quickly muffled as his skull popped through his face,
And asked, "Hey, where's the party? Am I late? Is this the place?"

D is for Didaskaleinophobia

(SCHOOL)

DJANGO'S FIRST DAY OF SECOND GRADE was awful. The classroom smelled like a dirty hamster cage and a classmate chuckled at his cartoon backpack (thanks, Mom). Their new teacher shouted, "Only HALF of you will survive this class!" A little dramatic, Django thought.

An oblong boy in a red football jersey repeatedly slammed his desk back against Django's, snorting each time Django's pencil fell to the ground, until the teacher finally noticed and sent the boy to the principal's office.

The rest of the day was so bad, I won't even describe it here. Django finally asked to be excused, took a small paper hall pass from his teacher, and proceeded to the bathroom where he cried quietly in an empty stall until the final bell rang.

The next day, the oblong boy was gone. Sick, Django hoped. But the boy didn't come back the next day. Or the next. As days went by, Django noticed more and more kids were sent to the principal's office, but no one ever seemed to return.

After a month, the classroom looked uncomfortably lean. Django suddenly recalled his teacher's ominous warning: "Only HALF of you will survive this class!" Django chuckled nervously.

"NO LAUGHING!" his teacher shouted, and with a stern, wrinkled finger directed him to the principal's office. As Django neared the office, he heard struggling and muffled screams inside.

"Go on in..." a lanky hall monitor said, smiling. His teeth were jagged and layered like a shark's.

Django fled down the hall, past the office. "NO RUNNING!" the hall monitor screamed, chasing after him. Django dove into the nearest bathroom. He searched his pockets for anything to defend himself.

The hall monitor burst in. Django nervously held out the crumpled bathroom pass from his first day of school. The hall monitor examined the pass, then snorted, "Well… hurry up!"

Django locked himself inside a stall, unsure what to do. Maybe he could escape once the hall monitor left? If he left? Maybe there was a window? What were his options? Django waited... and waited... and waited.

CASEY WAS LATE FOR CLASS. She'd missed her alarm (again) after forgetting to charge her phone (again). As she attempted to run six blocks in six minutes, a rainstorm suddenly occurred.

"Great," she said, stumbling through puddles. "Just what I needed!" Or at least, she WOULD have said that, if she wasn't cut off by 100 million volts of lightning striking her.

Casey woke up in the hospital feeling... pretty good, actually. Energized. She wondered how long she'd been asleep. Casey grabbed her cell phone, forgetting it was dead. "C'mon you, WORK!" she commanded.

Suddenly, the phone powered on. "Oh! Looks like you've got some juice left." The battery read 5%. Then 10%. Then 20%. "That's strange..." she said. Casey reached for a lamp, but it turned on before she touched it. "And so is that," she said, suspiciously.

On a hunch, Casey pointed at the TV and it sprang to life. She swiped her hand left and the channel changed. Casey stood up in her hospital bed. "This. Is. AWESOME!"

On campus that week, Casey used her newfound abilities to impress the other college students. She jump-started broken cars, added unlimited credits to the arcade games, and made the vending machines barf out all their candy. Casey was becoming pretty popular.

Then one day, while walking back to her apartment, Casey suddenly felt woozy. She heard a beeping and traced the sound back to her left hand. In the center of her palm, a small yellow 10% flashed.

"Weird," said Casey. The numbers changed to 9%. Then 8%. "Wait, what?" Casey asked, now worried. (7%) "How do I...?" (6%) "Where do I recharge??"

Casey began frantically searching for a plug. (5%) Or some batteries. (4%) ANYTHING! (3%) "HELP!!!" Casey screamed.

As her vision went black, she desperately felt the walls for an electrical socket. (2%) "Can anyone help me??" (1%) "PLEASE!!!" (0%)

F is for Frigophobia

(FREEZING)

"I'M NOT C-C-COLD!" Charlie said, throwing off her coat.

"I can SEE your teeth chattering!" teased her brother Albert. "Yeah, stop pretending you can stand the cold," mocked her other brother Austin. "You can't." They laughed as they skated out onto the lake.

Charlie hated them, but she knew they were right. Even after six winters here, she had never gotten used to the cold.

Charlie looked down at her coat with disgust. I don't need you, she thought. I'm only cold because I LET myself be cold! With shaking hands, she began peeling off each of her layers.

The boys noticed their sister's suddenly skinny frame and skated back. "Knock it off, twerp." "Yeah, put those back on before you freeze."

"I feel f-f-fine!" Charlie said defiantly. "Why? Are y-y-you guys cold?" The boys scoffed and headed inside. But truthfully, Charlie had never felt so cold in her life.

Over the next few weeks, Charlie continued her frigid rebellion. She wore T-shirts and sandals, sunbathed and ate popsicles. Her brothers demanded she stop, but she refused. In the battle of Charlie vs. Winter, she would be victorious!

Eventually her skin began turning white, her hair froze together, until one day… Charlie no longer felt cold. She ran home triumphantly to inform her family that she'd beaten the cold! She told her mother, her father, and her brothers, but for some reason... none of them could see or hear her.

Charlie tried reaching her family (unsuccessfully) for months. As the weather warmed, she fell into a deep, black, dreamless sleep. Charlie woke nine months later, when it was winter again, only to try again.

This continued for years. She watched her brothers grow up, get married, raise kids, and move away. She watched new families move into their home, grow old, and leave as well.

She watched for years, decades, centuries, no one able to see or hear her, until one year very far in the future when winter didn't end. It was very quiet. There were no more people, and Charlie was alone. Forever.

But she wasn't cold.

G is for Glossophobia

(SPEAKING)

KATYA'S SPEECH WAS A DAY AWAY and she STILL didn't have a topic picked out. Sure, there were tons of things she COULD talk about (and get teased about), like her top cartoons (BABY!), her book collection (NERD!), her favorite foods (FATTY!), or her stuffed animals (WEIRDO!). All she could think of was how hard it was to speak in public, which... might be the perfect topic?

The day of her class's speeches, Katya listened to the other kids talk about their pets, their hobbies, their dream jobs (why didn't THAT occur to her?). She clutched her notes so tightly, they began to tear at the edges.

Then after what felt like hours (DAYS!) and Jasmine Jones talking about her huge shoe collection (WHO CARED!) it was finally Katya's turn to speak.

Katya stepped up behind the podium. A hundred uninterested eyes leered back. She took a deep breath. "My topic is..." Someone coughed. "M-my topic is speaking. I mean, public..."

Someone laughed. Katya froze. Another chuckle. You idiot, why did you think you could do this??

The laughter grew. Katya wanted them to be quiet. The staff tried to calm the kids, which made them even louder. Shut up. Shut up. Shut up! "SHUT UP!" Katya screamed. Then it was silent.

Katya peeked over the podium and saw everyone trying to talk, but unable to make any noise. She chuckled, then immediately felt bad as her tiny laugh carried across the otherwise quiet room. People were silently sobbing, hugging, and phoning confused loved ones.

Katya looked at her notes. She needed to finish. She had the room. She cleared her throat. "My speech today... is on my fear of public speaking."

The audience watched intently as Katya delivered, as confidently as she could muster, five minutes and eight note cards on why it was difficult for her to speak in public. When she finished, she said, "Thank you," and the previously silent audience erupted into booming applause.

They began chanting Katya's name. And for the first time in her life, she didn't mind the attention. In fact, it felt great.

H IS FOR Hormephobia

(BEING SURPRISED)

JULIE WAS EASY TO SCARE (to scare), her classmates knew this well.
They'd sneak behind and startle her with unexpected yells,
(which kept her in her shell).

Until one day a voice (a voice) whispered in her ear,
"You shouldn't take that from them, THEY'RE the ones who need to fear,
(so here's the deal, my dear)."

The voice outlined a plan (a plan) to take revenge upon
The rotten teenage miscreants who treated Julie wrong.
(He claimed they'd soon be gone).

The voice asked just one thing (one thing) of Julie in exchange.
"Don't ever look upon me, as my countenance is… strange."
"Agreed," the girl proclaimed.

The two pursued each kid (each kid) who'd treated her unkind.
And each screamed at the sight of Julie's partner, terrified
(some even lost their mind).

Julie turned to thank (to thank) the voice behind her head.
It tried to warn her, "Don't look back!" It never wished her dead.
Julie's eyes went wide with panic, fear, despair, and dread…

Don't look back.

I is for Iophobia

(POISON)

THIS WAS A BAD IDEA, Faye thought, as she watched her brother mix vials of unlabeled liquid in their father's lab. "D-do you know what you're doing?" she asked, the empty mug trembling in her hands.

"Of course!" said Eli, pouring a neon liquid into his sister's mug. "Now drink up!"

Faye sniffed the bubbling liquid. It smelled like fabric softener poured over burnt toast. "How do I know this won't kill me?"

Eli made a PFFFT sound. "Please. This is SCIENCE, not witchcraft. And YOU'RE the one who wanted to be more popular. So… DRINK UP!"

Faye was relatively sure her brother's potion would kill her, but her life was pretty dull anyway, so what was there to lose? She squeezed her nostrils shut and guzzled down the bubbly liquid, then let out an involuntary (and embarrassing) belch. "Welcome to being cool," Eli said with a smirk.

At school the next day, Faye felt... more confident? Less shy? SOMETHING was different. In home room, no one made fun of her outfit. In chemistry class, Jeff (DREAMY) Davidson asked her to be his science partner. At lunch, Sarah (POPULAR) Peterson invited her to sit at the cool kids table. And by 2:15pm, Faye was friends with nearly everyone in her grade.

Faye ran home to tell Eli the great news. "Your potion worked!" she yelled happily.

"Actually, it was just random drinks from the fridge," Eli said. "You became popular because YOU believed in yourself." Faye smiled to herself. Then their father burst into the room, holding a pair of empty vials. "Kids! Please tell me you didn't drink anything from my fridge!"

As Faye and Eli jinxed on asking, "WHY?" Faye noticed the room was suddenly growing... or maybe she was shrinking?

Her brother and father watched in horror as Faye's teeth fell out, her ears melted off, her eyes sunk back into her head, and soon she was an oozing, bubbly puddle of flesh soaking into the shag carpet. Their father pointed an angry index finger at his remaining child.

"Fix this, Eli, or you're GROUNDED!" Then their father stormed out of the room, slamming the door behind him.

J is for Juveniphobia

(CHILDREN)

FRANKLIN COULDN'T STAND KIDS. Which was unfortunate, given that he worked as a school janitor.

He couldn't stand how kids played, how they walked, how they ate lunch, and especially how they would ask him questions anytime they saw him working in the yard.

Franklin didn't remember his own childhood, but he was pretty sure he was never quite so annoying as the kids at this school.

One day, a cheerful boy under a tattered baseball cap felt particularly inquisitive. What did Franklin do with all the trash? Did he live at the school? Was there a Mrs. Janitor? Did he eat homework?

Franklin couldn't stand it! He grabbed the boy, threw him into the tool shed, and locked the door. That'll teach him! Annoying little brat.

Almost immediately, Franklin felt bad and unlocked the shed to release the boy... but it was empty. Huh. Franklin shrugged and went back to his work.

The next day, a frustrating pair of girls in pastel dresses refused to leave until Franklin revealed how he kept the windows so clean.

He grabbed one of the girls, flung her into the tool shed, then sent her horrified friend in after her, slamming the door behind them. Just as before, Franklin soon felt awful for his actions. And just as before, when he opened up the shed, no kids were inside.

Over the next few weeks, Franklin sent over a hundred kids into the tool shed. He didn't know what was going on, but he appreciated being able to clean the windows, fix the doors, and mow the lawns in peace. Eventually the school was empty of all kids and Franklin felt intense regret.

He confessed to his supervisor, who looked confused. "Franklin, what kids?" He put his hand on Franklin's shoulder. "There haven't been any kids at this school since the fire twenty years ago. You know that." Franklin didn't understand.

"Maybe you should take some time off," his supervisor suggested. As Franklin returned to his chores, a squeaky voice behind him spoke up.

"Hey, mister! How ya keep the grass so green?"

ROACHES ARE VERY LUCKY INSECTS. Most people don't know this.
If you find a roach in your backpack, it means you'll do good at school.

If you find a roach in your wallet, it means you'll soon be rich.
If you find a roach at the playground, everyone will be your friend.

If you find a roach in your shoe, you'll travel somewhere interesting.
If you find a roach in your cereal, you'll have energy all day long.

If you find a roach on your toothbrush, your hygiene is impeccable.
If you find a roach in your comics, all the heroes will be victorious.

If you find a roach in your books – AAAAAHHH!
Did you see that?? A cockroach just crawled across this page!

Where did it go? Is it in your bed? Look under the sheets!
Did it fall in your hair? You better check, roaches love hair just like yours.

Maybe it's underneath your shirt. I think I saw it sneak under there.
No? Well gosh, I wonder where that roach went…

At any rate, roaches are very lucky insects.
And they're also very, very, very good at hiding.

Sweet dreams.

L is for Lygophobia (SHADOWS)

"**YOU'RE A LOSER, JEREMY!** And no matter what you do, you'll always live in my shadow!"

Caleb wasn't fond of his little brother. You could say he treated Jeremy like dirt, but Caleb never treated dirt that bad. Caleb slammed his door shut and tumbled into bed.

That night, he dreamt of dark figures chasing him. No matter how fast he ran, more and more figures sprang up until he was consumed by the darkness. Caleb woke up sweaty and annoyed.

On the walk to school the next day, Caleb noticed his backpack's shadow seemed darker than his own shadow. "Weird," he said.

In PE class, as the boys lined up for basketball, Caleb's shadow looked fainter than those of the other boys. His friend Tommy explained that "shadows vary in density based on their distance from the ground," or something (Caleb got bored and quit listening). But by lunch it was clear that Caleb's milk carton cast a shadow and he did not.

Caleb walked to the track to contemplate. Why did we have shadows anyway? Maybe this was a good thing. Now he could sneak up on people. It was practically a superpower!

He struck a hero's pose, then noticed something black behind his fingernails. He looked closer and saw it spreading, like ink staining fabric. Caleb screamed.

He ran to the nearby football team for help, but they ignored him. By now, the darkness was at his elbows. Caleb begged the coach for help, but when Caleb tried to grab him, their bodies passed right through each other.

Caleb ran to the hospital down the street. His entire body was pitch black now, a silhouette. He yelled for help, but none of the staff could hear him.

Caleb slumped against a wall, hopeless and out of ideas. Then he heard a faint crying nearby. He followed the sound to a nursery. All the newborn babies were sleeping, except for one hysterical boy. He noticed the baby had no shadow.

Caleb suddenly felt very small. He climbed into the crib, flattened himself against the blankets, and the baby grew calm.

"Maybe it's not so bad, living in someone else's shadow," Caleb thought. Then he closed his eyes and went to sleep.

M is for Melissophobia

(BEES)

"WORST. SPRING. BREAK. EVER," Simone muttered, arching her back against a tattered lawn chair.

The sun was getting obnoxious, so she slipped on her oversized sunglasses and tried to relax (as much as anyone could relax, after missing out on their friends' camping trip). Oh well, Simone thought. Vacationing on my hideous lawn will have to do instead.

She grabbed her lemonade and finished it with a few aggressive gulps. As she returned the glass to the table, she noticed a fat little bee just wiggling there.

"What's your deal?" Simone asked. The bee did not reply. "Go on, shoo!" she shouted, waving her hand. The bee didn't move. "Fine," Simone said, as she rotated her glass upside-down and lowered it down around the insect. "Enjoy your new prison. Dumb bee."

The bee tried to fly away, but repeatedly bumped into the glass. Simone chuckled, then leaned back into her chair and fell asleep.

When she awoke, it was already dark. "Dang, how long have I been asleep?" She looked over at the bee, still trapped under her glass. It was very still. She lifted the glass to release it, but the bee didn't move. Shoulda left when I told you, she thought, with only minor remorse.

She scraped the dead bee off the table with her glass, then closed her eyes once again. But a buzzing sound grew in volume all around her.

"Who's making that noise??" Simone demanded, raising up her sunglasses. But her frustration was replaced with terror once she realized the source of all the buzzing.

It wasn't dark at all. She was being circled by thousands of bees, so thick that they blocked out the sun. The bee tornado lowered itself down around her, just like she'd lowered her glass over the now-dead bee. Simone stumbled out of her chair and tried to run but got stung repeatedly.

As she collapsed on the grass, reeling from pain, the bees closed in on her, tighter and tighter. Simone couldn't escape. She couldn't scream. She couldn't even breathe.

Dumb bees.

N is for Necrophobia (DEATH)

IN HIS TEN YEARS OF LIFE, Jason had owned many pets. Two dogs, three cats, five hamsters, a gerbil, two snakes, six fish, and one grumpy turtle. He loved them all, they were his best friends, and eventually all of them died. Jason hated death and decided to get his revenge.

Late one night, Jason took his sister's second-favorite teddy bear and a pair of scissors, the sharp adult kind. He cut the bear in half then placed it on the floor, surrounded by dead bugs, for good measure. Jason grabbed his sleeping bag, hid behind his bed... and waited.

At precisely 11:03pm the room grew cold. Jason's breath escaped like tiny clouds. The shadows of his furniture drifted across the walls and a dark, tattered figure rose from the floorboards. "Death," Jason whispered, smiling like it was Christmas.

Death crouched to examine the cloven bear. "Thissss wasn't a living thing..." Death's voice sounded like cockroaches ground up in glass.

Then suddenly, Death was swallowed up by Jason's sleeping bag. Death thrashed about but Jason held tight until the bag stopped moving. Jason unzipped a corner and peeked inside. "What do you want?" demanded an icy voice.

"I want a friend," replied Jason. "Will you be my friend? I'll let you out." After a long pause, Death replied, "Deal."

Jason freed Death and over the next few days, the two became close friends. They went fishing, chopped down trees, and made omelets together. Death taught Jason to play chess and Jason taught Death to play video games. But soon it became apparent to Jason that Death was distracted.

"You need to go, don't you?" asked Jason. Death nodded as he rose. "Will I ever have a friend again?" Jason asked. Death paused thoughtfully, then plunged his staff into the ground.

Suddenly, tiny skeletons of cats and dogs and decomposing hamsters clawed their way to the surface and rushed to bury Jason in undead hugs and kisses.

As Jason, who would never be lonely again, struggled and laughed, Death quietly dissolved underground. He might've even been smiling.

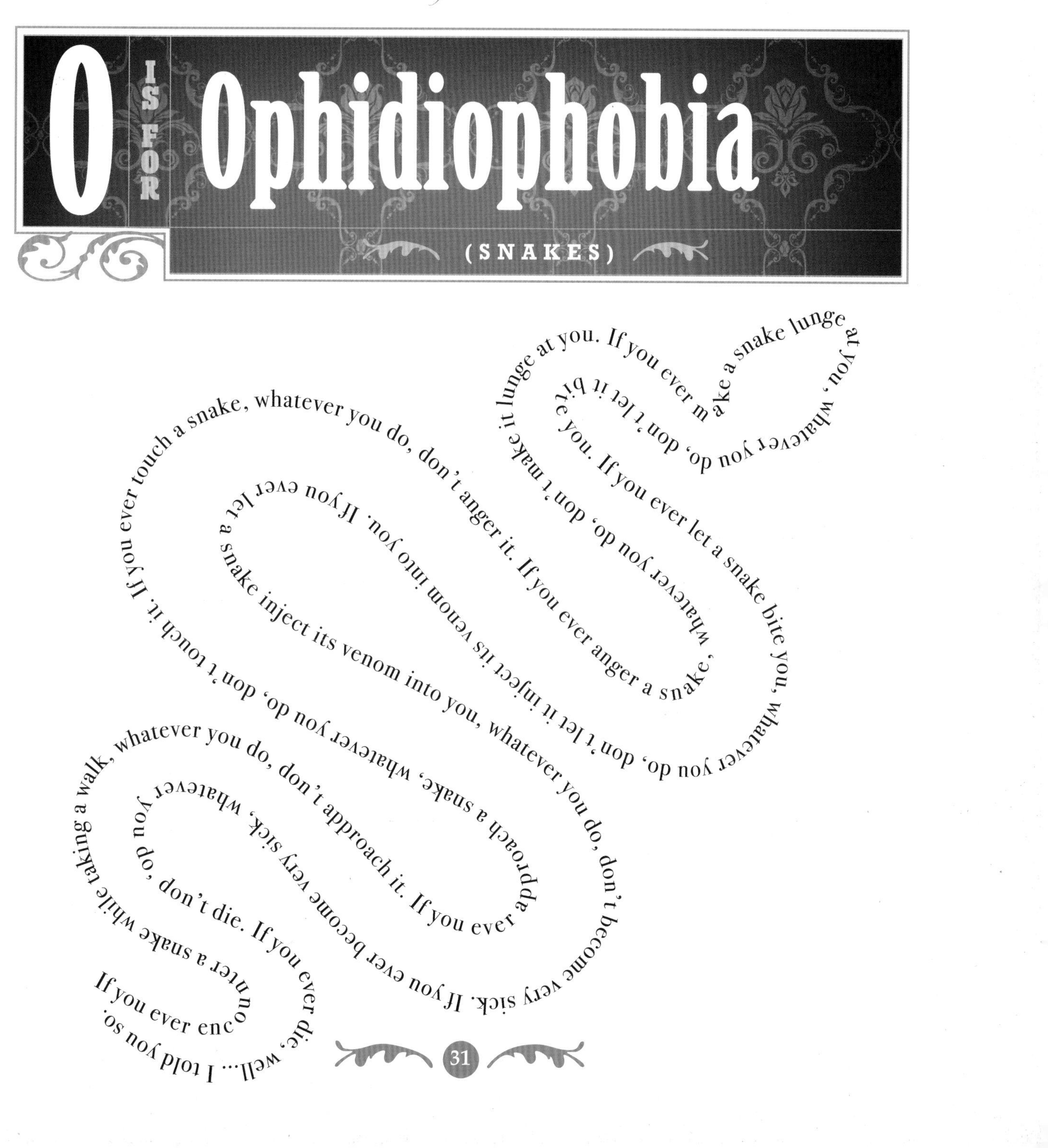
O IS FOR Ophidiophobia
(SNAKES)
If you ever encounter a snake while taking a walk, whatever you do, don't approach it. If you ever approach a snake, whatever you do, don't touch it. If you ever touch a snake, whatever you do, don't anger it. If you ever anger a snake, whatever you do, don't make it lunge at you. If you ever make a snake lunge at you, whatever you do, don't let it bite you. If you ever let a snake bite you, whatever you do, don't let it inject its venom into you. If you ever let a snake inject its venom into you, whatever you do, don't become very sick. If you ever become very sick, whatever you do, don't die. If you ever die, well… I told you so.

P is for Pyrophobia

(FIRE)

MELODY HATED CAMPING—the cold, the dark, the hiking—but most of all she hated how she'd, as expected, lost her friends and was now all alone on a snowy mountain at dusk. Just wonderful.

Melody cobbled together a pathetic little fire using twigs and leaves, resolving to sit and read and wait for her friends to find her, rather than get herself even more lost in the night. But soon, her tiny fire dwindled.

"Feed me all night," crackled the dying flames, "and I'll keep you warm till morning." Clearly she was hallucinating, Melody thought, but what did she have to lose? She mimed a handshake gesture over the flames and accepted the fire's offer.

"Feed me your book," the fire said. Melody knew she'd be bored, but bored was better than dead. She tossed her book into the flames, which immediately grew, devouring the pages. As promised, the fire kept her warm, but an hour later it began to die again.

"Feed me your sandwich," the fire said. Melody was hungry, but she was even more cold. She took a final bite, then tossed her meal into the flames. The fire greedily consumed her offering, but once again its warmth was short-lived.

"Feed me your boots," the fire said next.

"But then I can't walk," Melody replied.

"It's too dark to walk anywhere," hissed the flames. She couldn't argue that logic. She reluctantly removed her boots and dropped them into the fire. Melody continued feeding the flames throughout the night.

"Feed me," the fire said again, shortly before the night was over. Melody smiled.

"I have nothing left for you, but it is almost morning now. Thank you for saving my life."

The fire crackled angrily. "That wasn't our agreement!" The fire flung embers onto Melody's pants, which immediately caught fire. She struggled to put the flames out as they raced up her shirt. "Feed me ALL NIGHT and I will keep you warm till morning," the fire howled at her.

When morning finally came, all that remained was a large pile of ash. Melody's friends walked by, calling out her name. They noticed a tiny flame at its center, extinguished it with some water, then continued searching for their friend.

SHHHH! Cody tried to finish his math test (only 5 minutes left!) but he just couldn't concentrate with all the NOISE! Kim was rolling her pencil up and down her desk, Ethan kept scratching his head, Alice and Louise were both giggling, and Jake breathed loud as a jet engine. Hadn't these people ever taken an exam before?? Cody couldn't stand it. He got up onto his desk, took a very deep breath, and shouted, "QUIET!"

His teacher didn't appreciate the outburst and gave him two days of detention. On his walk home,

SILENCE! Excuse me, that was rude. On his walk home, Cody growled, "I just want to go somewhere quiet where no one will make any noise!" As he said this, Cody's foot caught on a tree root, causing him to trip and fall down a deep, dark well. His left knee got pretty banged up in the fall. High above him, he could see a ring of light pouring down into the well. Cody wondered how he'd get out

HUSH!

But can I just finish this story? I'm sure the readers would like to find out whether Cody is able to

SHUT UP!

Okay, fine.

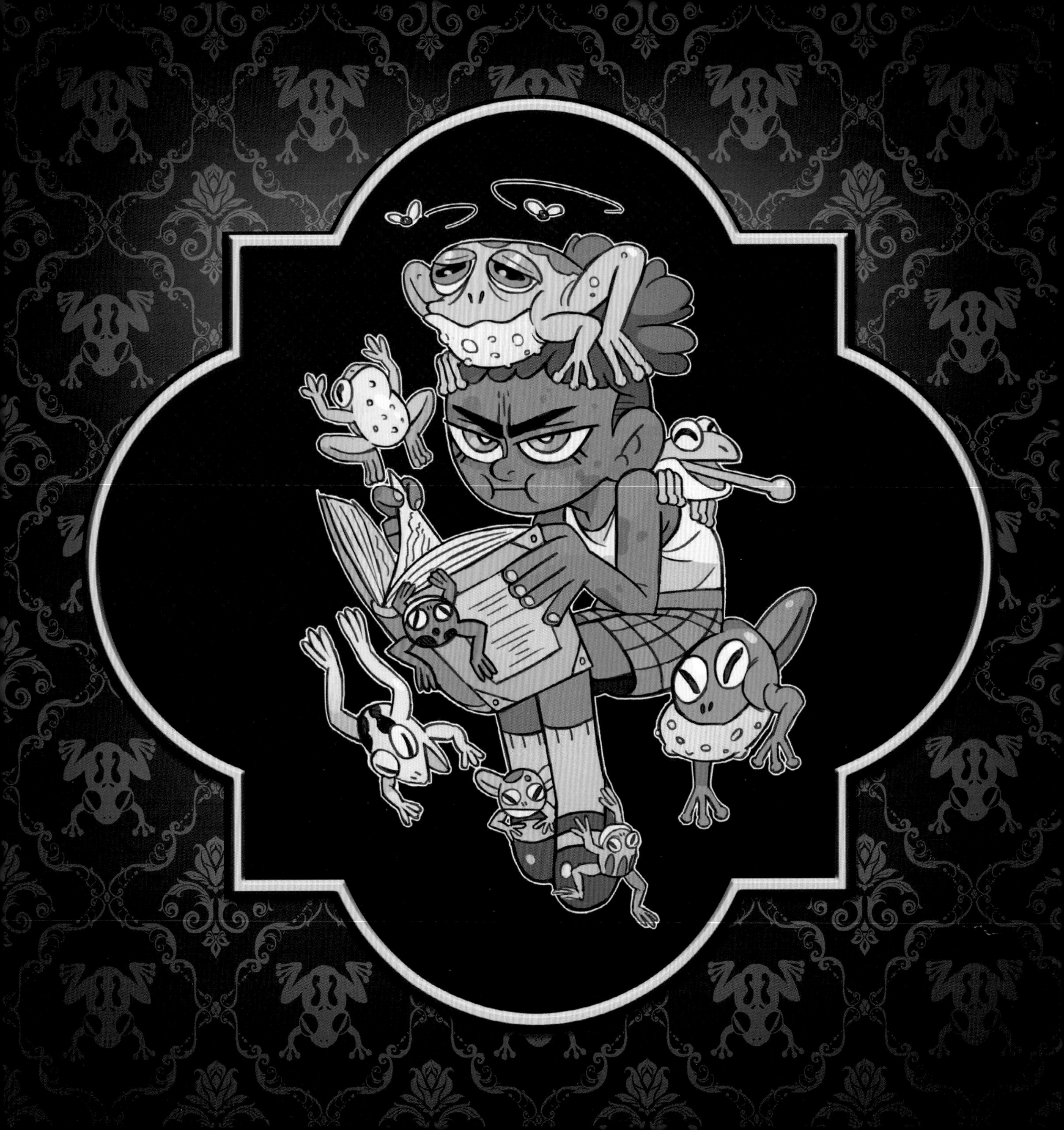

R is for Ranidaphobia (FROGS)

"KISS THIS FROG or we'll BURY you in this swamp!"

Aimee held Noel tightly by her hair as Kylee raised a soggy, tired-looking frog up to her face.

"DO IT," the girls demanded, snickering and snorting. Noel sighed and reluctantly pressed her lips against the frog. It felt like wet, slimy oatmeal. What a lousy first kiss, Noel thought.

Aimee and Kylee squealed with delight and ran off. Noel wiped her mouth, collected her muddy textbooks, made sure not to cry, and headed home.

The next morning, Noel felt sick. She ran for the bathroom but tripped over something. She looked down to see... green, webbed toes?? Noel opened her mouth to scream but a long, pink tongue shot out instead, breaking her lamp.

Her mother rushed in and, upon seeing a frog (Noel) on the floor, quickly shooed her away with a broom. Noel dove into her brother Eric's backpack and ended up hitching a ride to school.

At lunch, Eric reached for a ham sandwich with mustard but pulled out a plain frog instead. The lunchroom went wild.

Noel hopped through a sea of grabbing hands and stomping feet, out of the cafeteria, behind the school, and back to the swamp where it all began. Noel sat muddy and sad until she heard familiar giggling.

"DO IT, Aimee!" Kylee picked up Noel and shoved her in Aimee's face. Aimee gave the frog a reluctant kiss, then the girls ran off, amused and disgusted (respectively).

"You're such a JERK, Kylee!" whined Aimee.

Suddenly, Noel could feel her fingers again. And her toes. And her hair. And she realized she was no longer a frog. Noel breathed a deep sigh of relief, which was soon replaced by a sneaky smile upon realizing what Aimee would be going through the next day.

S IS FOR Scopophobia

(BEING WATCHED)

WENDA WAS PAINFULLY SHY. She hated people looking at her, speaking to her, or really even acknowledging her. To help her open up, Wenda's parents convinced her to start babysitting. She didn't really enjoy this, but the kids were nice enough, and she liked the extra money she earned.

One Saturday, Wenda was hired to watch Alan and Angela Jeffries while their parents went to the movies. The Jeffries' house was old, huge, and made creaking noises under the night's wind. But Wenda had heard that old houses made sounds, so she tried not to notice as she fed the kids dinner, bathed them, read them bedtime stories, and put them to sleep.

As Wenda returned to the living room, she heard a "tap, tap, tap" on the window. She turned and saw a dark face with big, bright eyes. She gasped, but on closer inspection, saw only tree branches scraping against the glass.

Wenda plopped down on the couch and explored the TV channels, when she heard it again—tap, tap, tap. She turned and saw a face in the glass door! But before she could scream, the face was gone. Did she imagine it?

Wenda went to check on the kids. They were fast asleep. Then she heard from the skylight above—tap, tap, tap. She looked up and once again saw a grinning face.

Wenda raced through the house, terrified. Every window she passed, she heard the same taps, and caught a glimpse of the same creepy face.

"GET AWAY!" she yelled, hurling a wax apple from the dining table through one of the windows. Glass shattered across the floor.

"LEAVE ME ALONE!" she screamed as she threw whatever objects she could find through every window in the house.

When Mr. and Mrs. Jeffries came home, they were not pleased. Their children were crying and the wind howled through all the broken windows. Wenda tried to explain what had happened, but they sent her home without pay. Wenda's parents grounded her until she repaid the Jeffries for all the damage.

That night, Wenda lay in her bed, wondering if she'd imagined everything. As she drifted off to sleep, the wind outside picked up, and from the skylight high above her bed came a familiar sound— tap, tap, tap...

=15

T is for Technophobia

(TECHNOLOGY)

HERE ARE THE INSTRUCTIONS for your new PC, the most amazing computer the world's ever seen.

Press P for POWER to turn it on,
Press M for MUSIC to play a song,
Press G for GAMES to jump and blast,
Press S for SOLVE to do your math.
Press L for LACES to tie your shoes,
Press T for TIDY to clean your room,
Press W to WASH your body,
Press E for EXPEL to use the potty.
Press N for NAP to go to sleep,
Press F for FOOD when it's time to eat,
Press V for VOICE when you need to talk,
Press M for MOVE to stand or walk,
Press B to BREATHE so you don't die,
Press C to CONTROL everything in your life.
Enjoy all the things your computer can do,
It'll outlast everything (including you).

COMIX

U is for Uranophobia

(HEAVEN)

UNFORTUNATELY FOR LIAM, he was dead. Fortunately, he seemed to have ended up in Heaven.

Liam sat in the cloudy expanse wondering what to do next. A handful of small, angel-like creatures hopped over to him and asked, "How may we serve you?" Liam scoffed.

"So what is this place, Heaven or something?"

"How may we serve you?" they repeated.

"Okay, fine," he said. "Give me a copy of every comic book ever written, 100 gallons of soda pop, and a TV with endless movies." The next time Liam blinked, everything he requested was right in front of him. "Not bad," he said.

"How may we serve you?" they asked again.

Liam gave it some thought. "How about… Abraham Lincoln, Albert Einstein, and Thomas Edison?" Liam blinked and was surrounded by the three men. They had a long theoretical chat that ultimately bored and confused Liam, so he sent them away.

"How may we serve you?" the creatures asked again. Liam sighed.

"I wish my friends were here…"

When he looked up, all his best friends from school stood before him. "But... how?" Liam asked. "They're not dead yet." The creatures smiled.

"How may we serve you?" Liam became skeptical.

"Okay then," he said, cracking his knuckles. "I want a machine gun. And a bazooka." Liam blinked and both weapons were in front of him. He fired each one repeatedly (they didn't seem to run out of ammo). "I want everything on fire!" he shouted. The clouds all burst into flames. Everything he'd summoned previously began to melt. Liam got frustrated.

"You're doing it wrong!" he yelled. "This isn't how it's supposed to be. You're angels, you're only supposed to give me NICE things." The creatures giggled.

"Who said we were angels?" Liam suddenly felt scared.

"Of course you're angels… this is Heaven," he said nervously, backing away from the flames. The creatures laughed and hopped after him.

"Who said this was Heaven?"

V is for Verminophobia

(GERMS)

CAROLINE WASN'T AFRAID OF GERMS. If one of her friends dropped a chip on the floor, she'd pick it up and eat it. When someone's toy got too filthy to play with, she'd take it off their hands. If they'd had enough milk, she'd happily drink the rest. "Waste not, want not," Caroline always said. Her friends told her she'd get sick if she kept on like that, but she didn't believe them.

Naturally, Caroline got sick. The doctor told her, "It's probably just germs. Take these pills to get rid of them." But Caroline didn't need pills, she thought to herself. She wasn't afraid of germs.

Later that night, Caroline was eating cookies in bed when one of them rolled away. No problem!

She recovered the fallen cookie from under her bed. It was covered in dust and lint. As Caroline brushed the unwanted garnishes off her fugitive cookie, she saw something wiggling in her palm.

She ran to the bathroom for a better look, but under the bright lights she saw nothing. Hmmm... MAYBE it wouldn't be a bad idea to wash her hands before bed, she thought.

Caroline plunged her hands into the sink. Both hands immediately dissolved into germs of various size and color. But before she could scream, new germs crawled down her arms and reformed her hands, finger by finger. Caroline didn't understand—was she made of germs now?

She looked in the mirror and squeezed her nose between two fingers… then pulled it off! Just as before, a handful of germs rushed across her face to rebuild her nose. Weird.

Caroline suddenly remembered the pills her doctor gave her. Maybe they could fix this! She popped a pill in her mouth, swallowed it, then felt an intense stomach pain. Her body violently shook itself apart into hundreds of germs that fled across the floor, all trying to escape, before each vanished into nothing.

Well that's not good, Caroline thought, seconds before her brain dissolved.

"Caroline!" her mother called, entering her daughter's bedroom. "It's dinner time! Where are you?" But there was nothing left of Caroline to answer.

Her mother noticed a cookie on the ground. She picked it up, shrugged, and took a bite.

W is for Wiccaphobia

(WITCHES)

JUST BECAUSE Alexis dressed as a witch for Halloween DIDN'T mean she believed in witches.

"They're not real," she told her brother Matthew as they went through their candy spoils. "Of course they are!" Matthew asserted. "There's an old witch who lives in the woods near school." Alexis rolled her eyes.

"SURE there is..." Matthew threw a gumdrop at his sister.

"There IS! I'd bet all my candy on it!" That was a bet Alexis couldn't pass up.

The next day after school, they snuck into the woods. "So where is this witch's house?" mocked Alexis. Matthew pointed. Just ahead was a small, shadowy structure.

"S-see?" said Matthew. "Now let's get out of here!" He turned to run but Alexis grabbed his coat.

"That's just some old cottage," she said. "No witch, no candy." Matthew groaned as his sister dragged him inside. Dusty cages and baskets and old books were piled everywhere. Red candles dimly lit the room, but no witch.

"W-we should leave," Matthew said nervously.

Alexis was about to agree, when they heard cackling outside. "HIDE!" They dove under some furniture.

An old woman with greenish skin, a pointy nose, and a heavy black robe shuffled inside. The witch (if that's what she was) began snatching ingredients and tossing them into a large cauldron. She paused. "Where is my… MEAT?"

She yanked back a tablecloth, revealing Alexis. "THERE'S my meat," she wheezed, licking her lips.

Alexis screamed as the old witch dragged her by the hair toward the cauldron. Then, with surprising bravery, Matthew charged at them, knocking the witch into her own stew. The witch screamed and howled as she boiled away into nothing.

"SEE??" Matthew said, catching his breath. "A real witch!" Alexis laughed.

"What witch? All I saw was a hungry old lady. You're NOT getting my candy, Matthew." Matthew moped. "Awww, no fair..."

Then suddenly, the door slammed shut, the candles went out, and a deep, cackling voice could be heard in the darkness all around them.

"MEEEAT…"

TABITHA WANTED TO BECOME AN ACTRESS. So when her school held auditions for a new play, she acted her heart out and won the lead role! Well, more like second backup lead, behind Jackie (ugh) and Serena (UGH). The only way Tabitha would ever see the stage is if BOTH of them dropped out, which never happens. Sigh...

Tabitha's drama teacher suggested she help with costumes, so over the next few weeks, she poured her energy into creating the play's elegant wardrobe. But as the debut neared, she became resentful of Serena, who was cast in the lead over her. Tabitha stared at Serena's costume.

"It should've been ME!" she yelled. She kicked the mannequin, knocking it against a wall. Tabitha immediately felt bad. Luckily, the costume hadn't ripped, although the mannequin's arm was cracked. Phew…

The next day, Serena wore a thick, white cast on her arm. She'd apparently broken her arm the night before—just like the mannequin! With the play just days away, Jackie would have to replace her.

Later, while working on her costumes, Tabitha stared at the mannequin wearing Jackie's outfit and had a terrible thought. She walked over, casually twisted its ankle backward, then went home.

To Tabitha's dark delight, Jackie came in the next day with a twisted ankle. Now Tabitha would need to take the lead (YES!) She sang to herself as she put the finishing touches on Jackie's… no, on TABITHA'S costume.

She was so excited that, while reaching for fabric, she accidentally knocked the mannequin's head off. Tabitha quickly screwed it back on. That didn't count, right? It was only off for a second. She stared at the mannequin with worry.

That night, Tabitha couldn't sleep. Would something horrible happen to her now, too? It was probably all just a coincidence, right?

She heard something moving in the darkness of her bedroom. CREEK… She tried her lamp, but it didn't work. CREEK… She found a lighter and flicked it on.

Standing silently around Tabitha's bed were three mannequins from her school. They stared at her with dead, wooden eyes. A breeze from her window blew out the flame. CREEK...

PARKER WAS THREE YEARS OLD, and in his parents' opinion, that was just too old for a blankey.

As Parker's parents threw his blanket into the trash, he wailed and cried. That night, after his parents were asleep, Parker snuck down to the kitchen, opened up the trash, and retrieved his beloved blanket. Then he crawled back into bed and quickly, happily fell asleep.

In the morning, Parker's parents were not pleased. That blanket had been in the TRASH! Parker's parents once again took his blanket away, and once again Parker cried as his parents threw it in the garbage can.

This time, Parker's father bundled the trash up, walked it to the curb, and dropped it in the bin outside. "No more blankey!" his mother shouted at Parker with a stern finger.

That night, when it was very late, Parker snuck downstairs, opened the front door, and rummaged through the trash bags on the curb until he found his blanket. It had become soaked with food and juices. Parker hid his blanket away in his room, and his parents had no idea he'd retrieved it.

Each night after his parents fell asleep, Parker would sneak his prized possession out of its hiding place. And each morning before they woke up, he would hide it there again. It was a complicated process for a three-year-old, but well worth it in Parker's mind.

Over time, Parker's blanket became even more filthy. It began to smell, dirt and food got stuck in it, and it began to attract bugs. But Parker didn't care, because he was happy.

One morning, Parker's blanket was so filthy it became stuck to his body. As much as he tried, he couldn't pry it from his skin... which meant he couldn't hide the blanket from his parents!

When his parents came in that morning, they were horrified at the disgusting mess they saw. Parker's father tried unsuccessfully to peel the blanket off his son. His mother ran to the phone to call for help. But Parker was happy.

"Don't ever leave me, Blankey," said Parker. The crusty blanket wrapped itself even tighter around the boy's body.

"I won't…" it whispered back.

Z is for Zoophobia

(ANIMALS)

ALEXANDRA LOVED CARING FOR ANIMALS. She ran a small farm for very sick creatures (ones that wouldn't get better) and helped them live out their remaining days in happiness. It was sad whenever one of her animals passed on, but Alexandra was happy because new animals were always dropped off to replace them.

Until one day, when the city decided to close her farm. "It's important to help SICK animals," the notice read, "not DYING ones."

Alexandra was heartbroken. She appealed the city's decision, she filled out documents objecting to it, but she was overruled. She tried offering pet-sitting services instead, but no one trusted her. She tried to lure animals in from the forest, but none came.

Alexandra sat on her front porch, tired and sad, staring at all the tiny graves she'd dug and filled over the years. She missed her friends deeply.

Wracked with loneliness, Alexandra took a shovel and began digging into the graves, searching for the animals she'd put there… but she couldn't find any of them.

It began raining, and the rain filled the open graves. Alexandra felt cold and sick, but she continued digging into grave after grave. Why couldn't she find any of her friends??

Late into the night, after hours of digging without any results, Alexandra stumbled into bed. She felt hot and exhausted. She tried to sleep but spent the entire night shaking in a fever.

When morning came, Alexandra woke up, although she didn't remember falling asleep. To her surprise, she felt fine. She was no longer sick, no longer sore, and no longer sad.

Alexandra stepped onto her front porch and was overjoyed to see all the animals she'd ever lost, all jumping and playing in her yard. When her animals saw Alexandra, they ran to her and nuzzled against her legs, and put their heads under her hands to be petted and scratched.

Alexandra was happy, for the first time since her farm had been closed. She cuddled against her animals in a sunny day that never seemed to end.

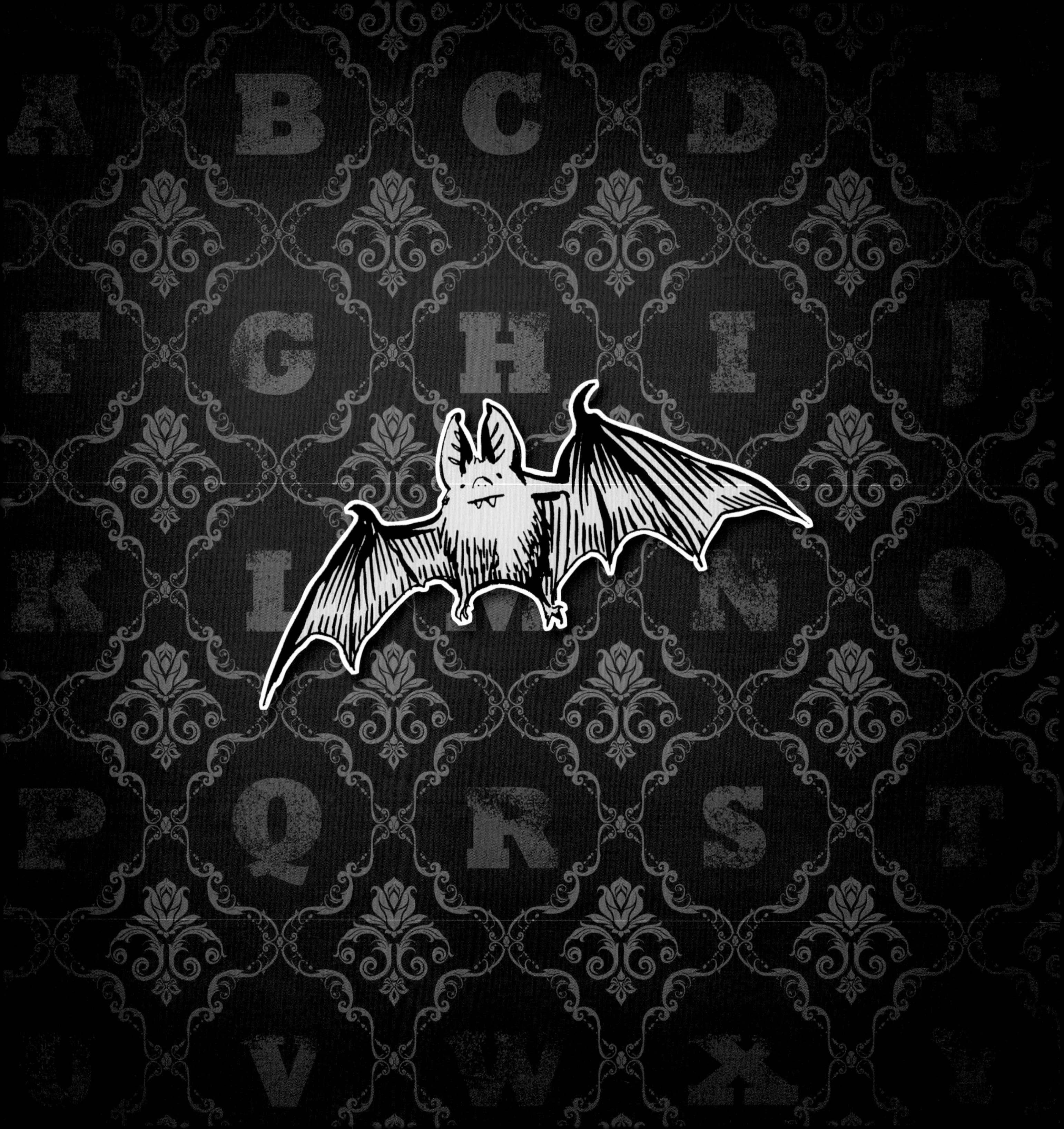

GUEST ARTISTS

The following section includes eleven bonus stories featuring illustrations by some of our favorite artists in the world. These artists range from animators to comic book artists to concept artists to video game developers. Each artist contributed their own spooky style to help bring these stories to life. We hope you enjoy them!

MJ

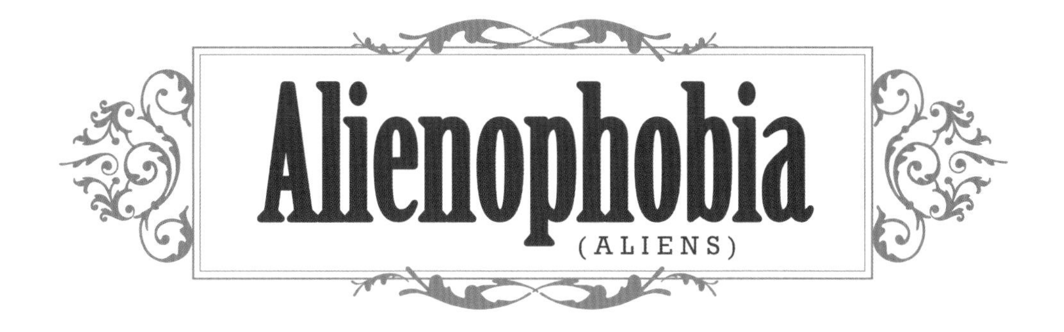

Alienophobia

(ALIENS)

LATE ONE NIGHT, Kellen opened his eyes to see a small, pale creature at the foot of his bed. It had no toes, few fingers, and two large, black eyes as shiny as an apple. The creature extended a hand and led Kellen downstairs, outside, toward an object so bright that all he could see was pure light.

"Where are you taking me?" Kellan asked. He soon found himself aboard a ship, surrounded by a dozen more identical creatures, who all made echoey chirping sounds as they examined Kellen. At one point he sneezed, which frightened half the creatures, and fascinated the other half.

Kellen felt the ship lift into the air and soon they were flying past stars and planets and asteroid belts, all visible through the ship's immense windows. Kellen again asked where they were taking him, but he couldn't understand their chirpy replies. Exhausted, he laid down and went to sleep.

Days passed on the ship, then weeks, then months. Kellen grew used to his tiny, saucer-eyed shipmates. He enjoyed their food and began to understand their chirping. Eventually, he stopped wearing his pajamas (everyone else was naked) and also stopped brushing his hair, which had begun to fall out (but who needed hair anyway?)

Kellen's eyes grew wider, allowing him to see through the dark of space, and he hunched over so often, in the too-short rooms, that his body began to shrink. Until many years later, Kellen looked just like everyone else aboard the ship.

Then one evening, Kellen (who now preferred to be called K-Lan) saw a familiar, blue planet in the distance. Their ship landed on the planet, a portal opened, and one of the creatures gestured for K-Lan to exit. K-Lan found himself on a farm, very much like the one he grew up on.

K-Lan spotted a large farm house. He snuck inside, crept up the stairs, and discovered a girl about his age (Molly) resting in her bed. Molly opened her eyes to see a small, pale creature at the foot of her bed, extending one hand, ready to take her on an adventure.

Athazagoraphobia

(BEING FORGOTTEN)

NATE'S BIRTHDAY WAS NEARLY OVER and not one of his friends had come to visit him. Not that an 18th birthday was all that special anyway. After all, birthdays were for kids. And Nate was (as of today) an adult. So who cared, right?

He decided to get out of his boring, empty house and grab some food from the noodle shop across the street. But after waiting in a booth for 15 minutes, no one took his order.

Nate went to the coffee shop next door and ordered a drink instead, but they never called his name. Eventually, he decided to just head back home and end this awful day.

On the walk home, Nate passed a Curiosity Shop that he'd, curiously, never noticed before. He decided to buy himself a birthday gift. He spent the next hour rifling through baubles and trinkets until the shop's lights turned off. Nate checked his watch, surprised by how late it had become.

He ran to the front door, but it was already locked. The owners must have forgotten he was there. He rattled the windows and shouted, but no one heard him. It was very dark and very quiet.

Nate spotted some light peeking out from the back of the store. He followed it to a small door, about half the size of a normal door. Light bled through the cracks all around it. Still, a lit door must go somewhere, he thought to himself. So Nate opened the tiny door and crawled inside.

The door led to a tunnel that got smaller and smaller the further he went, forcing Nate to wriggle and squeeze his way through. Eventually he reached an even smaller door that led to a tiny room he could barely fit in at all. But Nate did fit, and he closed the door behind him.

Nate sat quietly in the tiny room, just big enough for him and nothing else. He couldn't remember why he was there. He couldn't remember where he was going. He couldn't remember his own name. He couldn't remember anything.

I'm sorry, I forgot… why am I telling you this story?

Autophobia

(BEING ALONE)

Vitas Varnas woke alone, as usual. He showered, put on his best suit, then drove to work. Vitas worked hard. He was friendly but ate lunch alone. When he finished his work, Vitas drove home, got undressed, and hopped into bed, hopeful that tomorrow would be better.

Chaetophobia
(HAIR)

LENORA IS BETTER THAN YOU. That might sound mean, but it's true. She's beautiful and smart and the best thing about Lenora, without question, is her long, wavy, silky hair. She'd been growing it out since birth, groomed and maintained but NEVER cut. Sometimes she'd style it into creative shapes like a boat or a windmill or the Eiffel Tower. Everyone was jealous of Lenora's hair.

Each morning, Lenora brushed her hair 1,000 times. But one day, her brush got stuck. Try as she might, she couldn't pull it free. She was already running late, so she wrapped her bangs around the brush (which actually looked pretty chic) and ran downstairs.

Unfortunately her father had made his inedible Cabbage Quinoa Soufflé for breakfast that day. Lenora couldn't be excused until she'd cleared her plate. So when her father wasn't looking, she dumped the food in her hair, wrapped a French twist around it, and cheerfully left the table.

Later at school, Lenora's hair got stuck in her chair. Rather than miss lunch, she buried the chair inside a chignon bun and ran off to join her friends. As the day went on, more and more items got stuck in her hair, and Lenora always hid them under some clever styling. By the end of the day, her hair was thick and massive and unbelievably gorgeous.

Erica (whose hair was just... okay) stopped Lenora on the way home. "Who are you trying to impress??" she demanded. Lenora sighed and rolled her eyes. Erica took a swing at her, but Lenora ducked, catching Erica's fist in her beautiful, bountiful hair.

"I'm stuck! HELP!" Erica screamed. Worried that someone might hear them, Lenora pulled Erica into her hair and covered her with a butterfly braid. Problem solved.

But Lenora's hair was so heavy now, from her chair and Erica and everything else stuffed inside, that it was difficult for her to walk. She stumbled under its weight and fell to the sidewalk.

Lenora struggled to get up, causing waves of hair to splash over her arms and legs, covering everything, until all that remained was a huge mound of hair, resting on the sidewalk. But it looked fabulous.

Chiroptophobia
(BATS)

DEEP IN HER CLOSET, surrounded by candles, Lara was summoning the dead. This wasn't her first attempt, though the dead never seemed to reply back. As she held a flashlight under her chin and recited heavy metal songs backward, she heard a THWACK against her window.

Lara slid it open, hoping to see a ghoul, ghost, or even zombie (played out as they were). But what fluttered inside was a screeching, flailing bat. It had hairy ears, deep black eyes, and a crusty, pig-like snout. It was the most beautiful thing she'd ever seen. Realizing her undead chat was a bust, Lara went to bed, leaving the window open for her new friend to come and go.

Lara woke to find two bats perched on her desk. "You found a friend," she mused, as the bats hopped about. When she returned home after school, there were six bats. Then twelve. Then so many she couldn't hazard a guess at their numbers.

The bats behaved more like pets than vicious blood-suckers. They snuggled with Lara as she slept, and flew off to hunt in the night, returning with dead rodents, bugs, and birds. Lara was flattered and used these gifts in her school dioramas.

Later the bats began brushing her hair, choosing her outfits, even making her breakfast (though they always burned the toast). Bats this smart must secretly be vampires, Lara thought. She briefly considered asking them to bite her on the neck but decided it would be rude.

Then one horrible, sunny afternoon, Lara returned home to find a huge circus tent over her house labeled "Killborn Exterminators." Her face went pale (even more than usual). She rushed inside through an untied flap. The thick gas made it hard to see or breathe. Lara coughed and stumbled up to her bedroom only to find it empty. Not a single bat. Her heart broke, then she passed out.

Lara woke in a hospital room. A pink, fluffy teddy bear sat at the foot of the bed. It was the worst thing she'd ever seen. Lara grabbed the bear to hurl it in the trash when she noticed two punctures on her wrist. A bite?

She felt her teeth with her tongue—sharper than usual. She set down the bear and smiled. Everything would be fine. She would join her friends soon enough.

Gerascophobia
(GETTING OLD)

AT HALF PAST ELEVEN, the chimes of the main hall clock woke Mildred from her evening nap. She put on her glasses, slung a sweater over her shoulders (it was particularly chilly), and she got to work. There wasn't much time but there was oh so much to do.

She distributed chairs and stools, hoping there would be enough (you could never really tell until they arrived). She carefully arranged each place setting. It wasn't the finest dinnerware, but Mildred cared deeply for each porcelain piece.

Just before midnight, Mildred put the kettle on, then sat upon her stool, clasped her hands, and waited. She felt tired and wished they'd come earlier, but that wasn't her decision to make. She spotted a smudge on one of the tea cups and hurriedly wiped it clean as the clock struck twelve.

The lights began to flicker out, leaving Mildred in complete darkness. But she knew the procedure, so she wasn't afraid. A blue flame erupted in her fireplace. It danced around briefly, before tiny blue wisps began floating out in pairs, up under the sheets she'd left out for them, filling each with the shape of a head, a torso, two arms, and no legs.

The figures danced around the room to inaudible music as Mildred sat patiently. Then they settled onto the various chairs, stools, or the mustard yellow couch.

Mildred got to her feet, stretching her back discretely, retrieved the kettle, then proceeded to pour tea for each of her guests. One by one, they would thank Mildred, then tell her about their life, and Mildred would tell them about hers.

It was never the same collection of visitors, although she'd occasionally recognize a voice, or one's posture, or a story detail. They drank tea and reminisced for hours, until light crept in between the curtains.

Morning always came too soon, Mildred thought. She rose to her feet, tired but happy, and waved goodbye to her visitors, as their flames extinguished and their sheets fell to the floor.

One of the last remaining guests asked another, "What's her story?" gesturing toward Mildred. "Poor old dear," the other replied. "She thinks she's still alive."

Hemophobia

(BLOOD)

Drip
Drop, drip
Flies your spit
Past your tongue and through your lips
You better run, you better hide, if you would like to stay. . .   . . . alive
Drip, drop
Drip
Drop, drip
Rolls your sweat
Off your forehead, down your neck
Find a hiding place to stay, and hope that it might go. . .   . . . away
Drip, drop
Drip
Drop, drip
Stream your tears
Out your eyes and past your ears
You're so afraid, it's almost here, it's everything you've ever. . .   . . . feared
Drip, drop
Drip
Drop, drip
Pours your blood
Mixing with the rain and mud
I can't describe what's going on, suffice to say it's very . . .   . . . wrong
And anyway, you'll soon be gone
Drip, drop
Drip

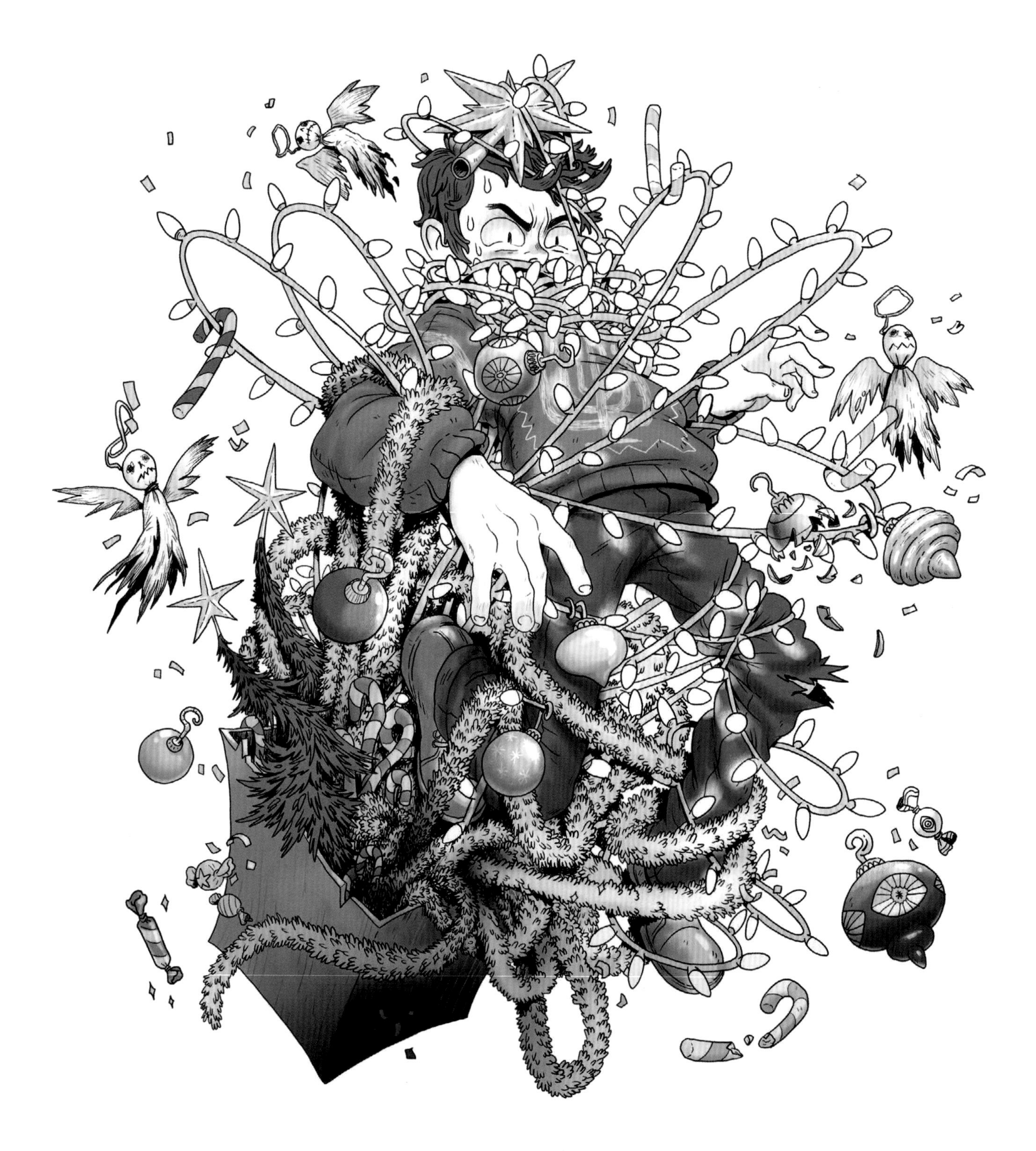

Heortophobia
(HOLIDAYS)

GATHER AROUND, CHILDREN, to learn the true meaning of Omnimas!

It started one December evening at a dreadful office holiday party. Norbert was doing his best to avoid his coworkers, but the room was too small. Norbert HATED holidays and knew this was just the first of many.

Soon he would be at parties for Christmas, Hanukkah, Bodhi Day, Kwanzaa, Winter Solstice, Festivus, and Boxing Day. That's when it struck him—everyone else had their own holiday, so why shouldn't he?

That night, Norbert created Omnimas, a holiday to replace all others. Did it involve presents? Nope. Singing? No way. According to Norbert, you just watched TV, ate snacks, then fell asleep.

The next day, whenever any of his coworkers invited Norbert to one of their parties, he'd reply apologetically, "I'm sorry, but I'm celebrating Omnimas that night. You've heard of Omnimas, right?" And they'd nod politely, even though they had not.

Norbert made it halfway through December when Dave from work knocked on his door. "Let's get this party started!" Dave shouted, shoving his way into the apartment. "What party?" asked a confused Norbert. "Omnimas, dude!" Dave said, grabbing the TV remote. Norbert wasn't happy about this, but he also didn't HATE Dave, so maybe having him around wouldn't be so bad.

An hour later, Florence from payroll came knocking. She'd heard about Omnimas and wanted in. Then Jake from accounting, Mickey from financial, and Doris from HR. Before Norbert knew it, his apartment was filled with people eating, sleeping, and watching TV. Norbert couldn't take it!

He ran outside but was mobbed by people asking about Omnimas. What shows do you watch? What snacks could you eat? Norbert was so upset, he stumbled backwards into a construction pit, impaling himself. And like lemmings, his newfound followers fell in after him.

He was annoyed, but as he lay dying, Norbert took comfort in the fact that he was done with holidays forever. And that, children, is why we celebrate Omnimas. Now watch TV, eat your snacks, and get some sleep.

SALT

Lachanophobia
(VEGETABLES)

CRISTINA HATED EATING HER VEGETABLES. And by that, I don't mean she'd just fuss and fidget, or push them around creatively on her plate. I mean she HAAAAAATED eating her vegetables.

Cristina's dinner plate shattered against the wall. "I'm NOT eating them!" she screamed. Her father said nothing, other than a deep sigh (which said everything).

"You eat your vegetables RIGHT NOW!" demanded her mother, under a stern finger. "They're GOOD for you!" Cristina broke another plate and was sent to her room.

That night, Cristina dreamt she was five inches tall. She lay on the kitchen counter, surrounded by vegetables as big as her. Her mother, now tall as a building, diced up onions, broccoli, tomatoes, and peppers for a stir-fry dinner. She casually snatched up Cristina, chopped her up into little pieces, then threw her daughter's remains into the wok to simmer with the other ingredients.

Cristina woke in a cold sweat! Not because she'd been diced and stir-fried, but because she'd just touched vegetables! She felt something in her hand... a piece of broccoli. Nice try, Mom.

She flung it across the room and went back to sleep. Later, Cristina heard a rustling at the foot of her bed. She turned on her lamp to see a large tomato idling on the blanket between her feet. "I'm NOT gonna eat these, Mom!" she shouted. The tomato slowly rotated, revealing an unsettling smile.

Cristina backed away from the vegetable (fruit?), which shuffled in her direction. "Good for you," it mumbled. She noticed more vegetables climbing onto her bed. "Good for you, good for you," they chanted.

Cristina tried to leap out of bed but a pair of red peppers held her arms. She tried to scream, but found her mouth stuffed with carrots and cauliflower, which crawled down her throat.

Cristina quickly passed out, her belly filled with joyous, dancing food. Later, her parents peeked in to find their daughter sleeping peacefully (they assumed), surrounded by half-eaten veggies.

"See?" said her mother, warmly elbowing Cristina's father. "I told you she'd come around."

MINDY HAD NEVER SEEN A GHOST, which was not unusual for someone her age, or any age really. What was unusual is how she desperately wanted to see one.

Although Mindy was only twelve, she'd been collecting haunted relics since she was six years old. (Can you think of anything you've done for half your life? I thought not)

She owned hundreds of totems, rings, masks, charms, beads, statues, and crystals, which was especially impressive because her allowance was only $5 per week (IF she cleaned her room and finished her homework).

Mindy once bought the bones of a tiny, unidentified creature from a local Curiosity Shop (though they smelled like fast food chicken bones). She once won an online auction for 37 letters written in 1913 between a boy and a ghost (both named Thomas). And her most prized possession was a small, mechanical doll that rolled its eyes back when wound up, mostly because it scared her sister.

But in all Mindy's years of collecting, through all her efforts to cast incantations and call forth the spiritual energy locked inside her supernatural treasures… nothing ever happened.

So when she turned thirteen, Mindy decided there were no ghosts in the world. She tried selling her collection online, but no one seemed interested. So she took her apparently-not-very-haunted trinkets to an empty parking lot and smashed them, one by one, until all the rings, charms, totems, and crystals blended together into a singular pile of metal, glass, and (probably) chicken bones.

Mindy started walking home when she heard a rumbling behind her. She turned to see the pile of ex-relics glowing green and rising into the air, as if dropped into a swimming pool (but upside down). The glowing mass grumbled at her, "WHY did you destroy our HOMES??"

Mindy wanted to run, but couldn't, unsure whether it was fear or the ghosts that froze her.

"Oh well," said the glowing mass as it floated toward her. "We guess we'll have to live… in YOU now!"

THANK YOU FOR PURCHASING your new VIDEO GAME. Below are instructions on HOW TO PLAY:

1. INSERT game cartridge into console and turn power ON.
2. If game does not start, REMOVE cartridge, BLOW inside it, then repeat Step 1.
3. After powering game on, press START BUTTON to begin gameplay.
4. Press D-PAD to run, press A BUTTON to jump, and press B BUTTON to fight.
5. Collect FRUIT and POWERUPS but avoid touching ENEMIES.
6. Touching an ENEMY will cause your character to take DAMAGE.
7. If YOU feel pain when this happens, don't worry. This is normal.
8. Taking too much DAMAGE will cause your character to DIE.
9. If you feel YOURSELF dying when this happens, don't worry. This is normal.
10. Allow your SPIRIT to float away from your body and ENTER the cartridge.
11. You may feel your HOPES and MEMORIES converting into DATA. This is normal.
12. Do not feel SAD or CRY. Every kid wants to be in a VIDEO GAME! Don't YOU?
13. There is no warranty, guarantee, or ESCAPE from this game. You belong to us now.

Thanks for playing.

BEHIND THE SCENES

AFRAID of EVERYTHING is a project that I began thinking about in the summer of 2015. I was inspired in part by the horror books I loved as a kid, and in part by having recently discovered the wonderfully creepy artwork of Matthieu Cousin, who illustrates most of the stories in this book.

I decided to work with the crowd-funding website Kickstarter to fund the production of my book. Doing this would provide me with the money I needed to pay all the talented artists who would be contributing, and it would also force me to actually complete the book, as hundreds of people would be waiting for their copies.

The Kickstarter campaign went very well, more than tripling our original goal, as well as generating a great deal of interest in this project and in the idea of producing real horror stories for kids again.

On the following pages, you'll find a collection of artwork by Matthieu Cousin and others, including rough sketches of some of the book's illustrations, and some of the artwork that Matthieu created for the Kickstarter campaign.

I hope you enjoy this peek behind the scenes at how we made this creepy book!

— Adam Christopher Tierney

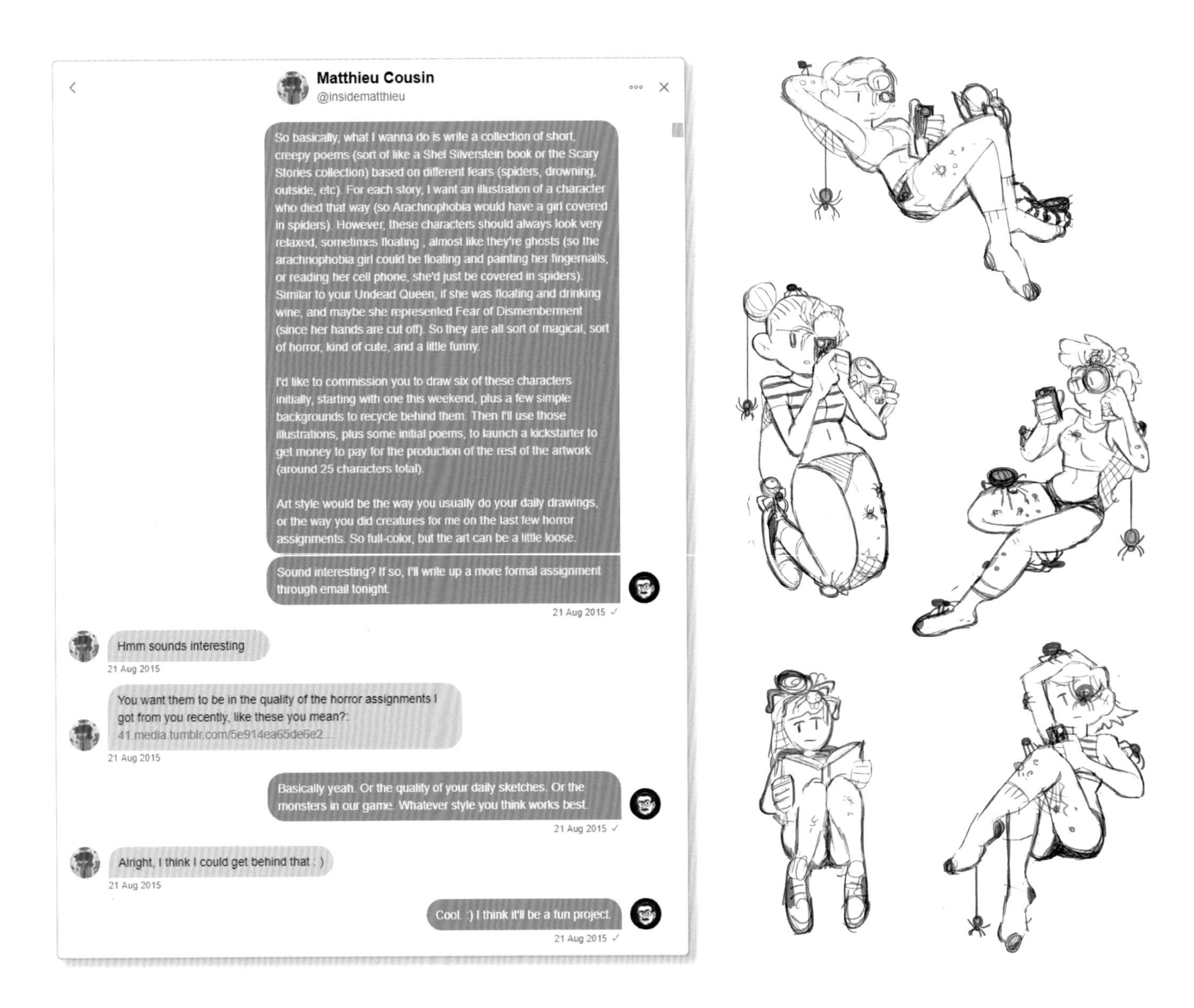

ABOVE IS THE FIRST CONVERSATION I ever had with Matthieu about this project, not in an email but in a private message on Twitter, funny enough. Matthieu liked the idea and immediately started on sketches for the main character in our first story (Arachnophobia), some of which you can see on this page. I would then use Matthieu's sketches as inspiration to write each story.

ONCE MATTHIEU FINISHED HIS ILLUSTRATION of our spider-plagued protagonist, I went to work on the book's design. The idea was to have overly-formal framing to juxtapose with the casual pose of the characters. Matthieu also designed a custom icon for each story, like the spider above, which we worked into the wallpaper design behind each character.

WE INITIALLY PRODUCED FIVE STORIES for the Kickstarter campaign plus the main cover image. A few weeks into the campaign, we produced another three stories to help promote the project. But the real workload would begin once the campaign wrapped, with Matthieu producing a total of 26 unique story images. Above are some of his rough sketches for those.

KICKSTARTER CAMPAIGNS ARE TYPICALLY very visual, especially when the project involves illustration. So in addition to the story images, Matthieu also produced several campaign-specific pieces of art, all using the same art style as the book. These illustrations were used on the main campaign page, in the campaign video, and in various backer updates sent out during and after the campaign.

AS PART OF THE KICKSTARTER CAMPAIGN's stretch goals, we decided to add ten bonus stories (which eventually became eleven). I wanted these stories to feel different from the 26 main stories, so we broke away from the A-Z alphabet theme, illustrated them in grayscale (rather than full-color), and most importantly we worked with a variety of guest artists that Matthieu and I love. Above are the rough sketches from some of these guest illustrations.

FINALLY, THIS PAGE CONTAINS miscellaneous imagery created for the book including portraits of me and Matthieu (by Matthieu), the signature sheet for signed copies, a postcard to promote the book at conventions, pre-campaign teaser images, my son Django acting spooky, and fan art by Manuel Samolo (who would later contribute to the bonus story section). Thanks for reading! We hope you've enjoyed this behind-the-scenes glimpse into the production of this book.

THE AUTHORS

Provided below is information on the unfortunate individuals who created this book.

ADAM TIERNEY is a video game developer, TV writer, and (now) scary book author. He lives in Los Angeles, CA with his wife Amy, his children Django and Nina, and as few pets as possible. Over the past fifteen years, Adam has directed dozens of video games (several of them spooky) and oversees business development at game studio WayForward.

MATTHIEU COUSIN is a character designer/illustrator currently based in Sweden. After finishing his studies in Malmö, he ventured into the land of freelancing, doing jobs for various projects such as games, books, and cartoons. Some of his previous clients include Disney TVA, Cartoon Network, Nickelodeon, and WayForward.

ILLUSTRATIONS BY MATTHIEU COUSIN

=15